WITHDRAWN

✳ Smithsonian

AUDREY and APOLLO 11

BY REBECCA RISSMAN
ILLUSTRATED BY JACQUI DAVIS

STONE ARCH BOOKS
a capstone imprint

Audrey and Apollo 11 is published by Stone Arch Books,
an imprint of Capstone.

1710 Roe Crest Drive
North Mankato, Minnesota 56003
www.capstonepub.com

The name of the Smithsonian Institution and the sunburst logo
are registered trademarks of the Smithsonian Institution. For more
information, please visit www.si.edu.

Library of Congress Cataloging-in-Publication Data is available on
the Library of Congress website.
ISBN: 978-1-4965-9862-2 (hardcover)
ISBN: 978-1-4965-9870-7 (paperback)
ISBN: 978-1-4965-9866-0 (ebook PDF)

Summary: Science-obsessed Audrey is a fifth grader in Houston,
Texas, who dreams of one day working at NASA, like her dad does.
Her dad, however, is nothing but discouraging. Audrey doesn't give
up, though. She's created her own model rocket. When it doesn't
fly, she figures out a way to fix it that ends up helping the Apollo
11 astronauts after they land on the Moon. Will Audrey's dad
come around? And will Audrey have a future in science?

Designer: Tracy McCabe

Our very special thanks to Margaret A. Weitekamp, PhD,
Department Chair and Curator, Space History Department,
National Air and Space Museum. Capstone would also like to
thank Kealy Gordon, Product Development Manager, and the
following at Smithsonian Enterprises: Jill Corcoran, Director,
Licensed Publishing; Brigid Ferraro, Vice President, Education and
Consumer Products; and Carol LeBlanc, President, Smithsonian
Enterprises.

TABLE OF CONTENTS

Chapter 1

Rocket Trouble

Audrey squinted at the sketch in her notebook. A carefully shaded Earth hugged one edge of the page. The opposite edge held the tiny, cratered Moon. She dragged her pencil one and a half times around Earth and then began to pull it toward the Moon in a long, curving path. She imagined that the very tip of her sharp pencil was a cone-shaped spacecraft, headed for the first-ever crewed lunar landing.

"Hi!" Audrey's mom said, poking her head through Audrey's door.

Audrey jumped, and her pencil jerked across the page. "Mom! You scared me!" She tucked the pencil into her messy ponytail.

"Sorry, kid," her mom said, peering at Audrey's drawing. "Hey, that flight path's looking groovy. Almost done?"

Audrey giggled. "Mom, stop saying *groovy*. It's embarrassing! And I can't finish if you keep interrupting me."

"Okay, okay," her mom said, smiling. "I used to have my science classes map out the first two Mercury flight paths."

"I know, Mom."

"It was pretty simple back then," her mom continued. "Just the launch, a big arc, and splashdown. Those missions only lasted fifteen minutes. Apollo 11 is going to be much longer. Buzz Aldrin, Neil Armstrong, and Michael Collins will be up there for eight whole days."

"I *know* all of that!" Audrey interrupted.

Her mom laughed and then paused. She tapped the pencil sticking out of Audrey's hair. "Groovy hairstyle, kid."

"Mom!" Audrey groaned.

Her mom chuckled and left the room.

Audrey turned back to her notebook. Just as she began erasing the pencil mark she'd made when her mom startled her, a tinny voice squeaked from under her curtains. "Audrey? Audrey, do you read me? Over."

Audrey grinned. She picked up the tin can dangling from a string through her window and pulled it tight before she answered.

"Roger. Over," Audrey said.

"There's been an emergency," the tinny voice reported. "Over."

Audrey gasped. "What's wrong? Over."

Her best friend's response came through the cup. "I found something neat! Over."

"Gary!" Audrey laughed, then said, "Okay, I'll be right over. Uh . . . over."

Audrey dropped the cup, untied her ponytail, and rushed down the hall, yelling, "Mom-I'm-going-to-Gary's-bye!" as she went. She spun around a corner and—"*OOF!*"

Audrey smashed into her dad and sent the thick stack of papers he'd been holding airborne. NASA-stamped letters fluttered through the air. A diagram of the lunar lander fell onto Audrey's shoes. A rocket launch sequence jammed itself under a doorframe.

Audrey's dad worked in NASA's Mission Control. He helped design and monitor the flights of the space missions. His official title was Flight Dynamics Officer, but everyone at NASA called him a FIDO. Audrey would give anything to be a FIDO when she grew up, even if it did sound like a dog's name.

"Sorry!" Audrey said. She dropped to the floor to collect the papers.

"Just leave them," her dad interrupted. "These are my notes for Apollo 11. I need to be sure they're put back in the right order."

"Apollo 11?" Audrey asked. Her face lit up. "That's perfect, I've got so many questions about—"

Her dad waved her off. "This isn't for you."

"But, Dad—"

"Audrey, I said *no*. Now go." She went.

Her dad used to tell her everything about working at NASA—the astronauts pranking one another, the arguments about how and when to launch different missions, and the frantic race to beat the Soviets to the Moon. Then, one day Audrey announced that she wanted to work at NASA too. From that moment on, her dad refused to talk about his job at all. Audrey couldn't understand it.

"Hey, Audrey! Why the long face?" Gary called from his front porch. He was holding a bright yellow piece of paper.

"Oh, it's just—" Audrey began, but Gary cut her off.

"Check this out! The first meeting is today. In fact, it's this morning!"

Audrey read the yellow flyer:

HOUSTON ROCKETEER CLUB MEETING

5th–8th Grade
11 a.m., June 16, 1969
Houston Public Library

She looked up at Gary. "Well, we'll be fifth graders this fall. Think we can go?"

"Of course." He grinned. "We'll bring one of our rockets to show that we know our stuff."

The two darted into Audrey's garage. Neatly organized on a shelf in the back were rows of model rockets. Audrey and Gary had been building them together since the third grade.

"Whaddya think?" Gary asked, grabbing a narrow black-and-white rocket. "Should we bring our *Mercury-Redstone*?"

Audrey shook her head. "It's got to be the *Saturn V*." She lifted the huge white rocket carefully.

"You sure?" Gary asked. "That kit cost five times as much as the others. If it breaks—"

Audrey interrupted. "The *Saturn V* is launching Apollo 11! Of course we have to bring it. And I promise I'll be careful."

Gary looked at his watch and jumped. "T minus twenty minutes until the meeting starts. Let's go!"

They climbed onto their bikes and sped to the library. By the time they arrived, they were both breathless and sweaty. They hurried through the library halls and found a door with a sign reading WELCOME, ROCKETEERS.

Gary opened the door and they stepped inside. The room was packed with tall boys. Audrey felt very small. She and Gary edged their way to a row of open seats.

"Must be mostly eighth graders, huh?" Gary whispered. "These guys are giants!" Audrey nodded, suddenly nervous.

"Who you calling giants?" a particularly large boy with thick red hair asked Gary.

"Oh, uh . . . it's just that . . . um," Gary stammered.

"I'm just messing around," the boy said. "You're right. Most of us are from the eighth grade Boy Scouts, Troop Fifty-Three. A couple of our fellas are having an issue with their *Gemini-Titan* and we were hoping to figure out a solution here."

"What's the problem?" Gary asked.

The red-haired boy gestured to some of his friends to join the conversation. "Well, kid. Let me put it this way: The last time we lit the ignition, the troop had to hit the deck. The thing was out of control!" The boys laughed.

Audrey scratched her chin. This sounded familiar. She'd once had a similar problem with a model rocket. One of her fins had been slightly crooked, and it had sent the rocket flying in a cattywampus path. She stepped closer to the group and said, "I bet I know what's happening."

No one seemed to hear her. "Hey," she said, a little louder, to their backs. "I think I know the issue. Have you checked your fins? They might be crooked!"

Still no one turned to look at her.

Audrey tried again. "YOUR FINS?"

No one reacted to her voice. "Gary?" Audrey tried. But even he didn't hear her.

She felt irritated. Were they ignoring her on purpose? Or had they heard her and just disagreed? That idea rattled her. What was going on?

Audrey turned to take a seat and wait for the meeting to start, but when she did, her shoe caught on a chair. She lost her balance and fell—right on top of their model *Saturn V*.

CRUNCH!

Audrey stared in horror at the broken rocket on the floor. Black-and-white pieces were everywhere. It was ruined.

"Ouch!" Someone chuckled cruelly.

Audrey looked up to see that everyone was staring at her. Their faces looked mean.

Another boy joked, "Who let the little girl in here?" The room erupted in laughter.

Her dad's words echoed in her mind: "This isn't for you."

Tears stung Audrey's eyes. She ran out the door.

Chapter 2

Liftoff

Whenever Audrey pictured the Rocketeer meeting, she winced. It had been nearly a month and the memory was still painful. First, everyone had ignored her. Then, she'd wrecked the rocket she'd made with Gary.

What a disaster! Audrey thought.

She shook the memory away and walked into the kitchen just in time to help her mom carry three foil-covered TV dinners into the living room. Audrey's six-year-old brother, Alan, counted them and then said, "Dad's working late again, isn't he?"

"Looks like it," their mom answered. "The guys running Apollo 11 are working overtime to get everything ready." She moved a stack of space books off the couch and took a seat.

Back when Audrey was a baby, her mom had tried to juggle teaching science with family life. But it was hard. After Alan came along, she had quit teaching. She planned to go back to work in a few years, so she was always reading to stay on top of the current science news. And lately, all the exciting news seemed to revolve around spaceflight.

Alan whined, "I wish Dad was here."

"Me too," Audrey said sadly. Then, her face brightened. "I wonder if he'd ever let us tag along at work. That could be fun."

Their mom's eyes widened at the idea. Then she turned to their television in the corner of the room. "Shh," she said. "The program is about to start."

Audrey looked at the TV. News anchorman Walter Cronkite sat behind a large desk.

"Good evening," he began. "We start in Cape Kennedy, Florida, where the countdown continues for the brave crew of Apollo 11. Today, July 9, 1969, marks one week until launch, and eleven days until the Moon landing."

Audrey's heart raced. It was nearly time.

The next week crept by. When launch morning finally rolled around, Audrey was giddy with excitement. Gary's mom invited Audrey's family over to watch it at their house. This was good for a couple of reasons. First, Gary was a pretty entertaining friend to watch space launches with. During Apollo 8's launch the previous year, he'd gotten so excited that he actually fell backward off the couch at liftoff. Audrey giggled just thinking of it.

She could smell the second reason it was good to be at Gary's. "Mmm. Did your mom bake cinnamon rolls?"

"Sure did!" Gary answered from his seat on the floor, inches away from the television. "Take a seat. It's about to start!"

Audrey, her brother, and her mom hurried to the couch. The TV showed the *Saturn V* rocket with the Apollo capsule on top. And a countdown timer displayed the time to launch: 2 minutes, 45 seconds.

Audrey felt her mom squeeze her hand. The screen switched to a view of the rocket's five enormous engines. The voice narrating the countdown sounded urgent. "Forty seconds away from the Apollo liftoff . . . thirty-five seconds and counting."

Audrey leaned forward. She held her breath. Her mom's grip tightened. The voice continued, "Twelve, ten, nine, ignition sequence starts,

six, five, four, three, two, one, zero. All engines
running."

Orange flames burst from the bottom of
the *Saturn V.* The rocket slowly heaved off the
ground.

"LIFTOFF!" Gary yelped. "WE HAVE
LIFTOFF!" He leapt to his feet with his arms up
in the air—and promptly knocked the platter
of cinnamon rolls off the coffee table.

Nobody paid any attention to the pastries rolling across the carpet. They were too focused on the TV. The rocket soared upward. Audrey cheered. Her mom clapped. Alan whooped. The mission had officially begun.

Audrey thought about the flight path she'd drawn in her notebook. Right now, the astronauts were on the very beginning of their journey. Next, the crew would orbit Earth. On the second loop around the planet, a set of engines would fire them toward the Moon. Then, while rocketing through space, the components of their spacecraft had to be rearranged.

Apollo 11 had launched with the command module, called *Columbia*, and lunar module, called *Eagle*, separated by the service module. They'd separate the *Columbia* from the cluster, rotate it, and then steer it back to dock with the *Eagle*. This spindly combination would then travel for three days until it could enter

the Moon's orbit. It was a distance of about two hundred forty thousand miles. Then, if everything went exactly right, they'd try to land on it. It was an extremely complicated flight plan. But Audrey thought they might pull it off. Goose bumps prickled her arms at the thought.

When Audrey's dad came home that night, he looked tired but happy. He dropped his briefcase on the kitchen counter, then went out into the backyard where her mom was relaxing in a lounge chair. Audrey followed him outside. She looked up to see stars glimmering in the darkness. The Moon was a sliver in the sky. She pictured the Apollo 11 crew in their spacecraft—a tiny speck in that giant black expanse—and grinned.

"Dad! Tell me everything!" Audrey blurted out. "What was it like? How's the crew?"

Dad turned, surprised to see her. "Audrey? What are you doing up?"

"I'm not tired!" she said. "I want to hear about the mission. I'm dying to know how—"

"Not now," her dad said firmly, pointing toward the house. "Bed."

Audrey turned sadly and shuffled inside. On her way to her bedroom, she saw her dad's briefcase. She remembered the stack of papers she'd sent flying in the hallway. Maybe he'd brought them home again.

An idea hit her: If her dad wouldn't tell her about his day, maybe she could read about it. Of course, he'd be furious if he found out she was snooping through his things. But . . . Audrey glanced out the back door. Her parents were still talking. If he never found out . . . why not?

Now was her chance.

She opened the briefcase and grabbed the first thing she saw, a thick booklet titled *Apollo 11 Flight Plan*. Audrey had heard her dad say that flight plans covered every detail of space missions, from launch to splashdown. She grinned.

Audrey hurried to her bedroom and opened the booklet. The text inside was dense and complicated, but she could make out little bits here and there. Then she saw something scrawled on the edges of the pages for the first day of the mission. It was her dad's handwriting.

On one page, he had written: "Crew relaxed. Launch to proceed." The next page read: "9:32 a.m.: Liftoff. All A-OK. Big smiles inside Mission Control."

More notes followed. Audrey read about the weather, the rocket speed, and the conditions inside the capsule. Her dad's notes were short but descriptive. It was almost as though she were reading his diary entry for the day.

A few pages later, her father had scratched: "12:22 p.m.: TLI. Here we go!" Audrey knew that TLI stood for translunar injection. That was the moment when the spacecraft was fired out of Earth's orbit and toward the Moon. The bottom of that page was stained and wrinkly. It looked like someone had spilled coffee on it. Audrey wondered if her dad had been so excited that he'd knocked his cup over onto his flight plan. She chuckled thinking about it.

Audrey closed the flight plan and listened at her door to see if her parents were still awake. The house was quiet. She scurried to the kitchen and returned the flight plan to her dad's briefcase.

She fell asleep smiling. Her dad might not want to talk about the mission with her, but she could hear his voice in her head saying, "Here we go!"

Chapter 3

Rocket Science

"How long till the Moon landing?" Audrey asked for the hundredth time that morning. She and Gary stood in a field behind her house setting up a model rocket launch pad.

"Three hours and thirty-two minutes," Gary answered with a sigh. July 20, 1969, would surely go down in history as the world's longest day. Just then, a group of boys approached. Audrey recognized them from the Rocketeering meeting. *Ugh*, she thought. *The Boy Scouts.*

"Hey, Gary!" one of them said. "Whatcha launching?"

Gary pointed to the small, sleek rocket in Audrey's hands. "It's called the *Streak*."

"Oh, that's cute," one of the boys said. Then he looked at Audrey. "Looks like a good starter rocket."

Audrey clenched her jaw. "It's not a starter rocket. And for your information, it can go two thousand feet into the air."

"Well, then, we'd better step back." The boy smirked.

Audrey scowled and set the rocket onto the launch pad. She connected her launch controller to the engine's igniter wires, and then backed up. Gary inserted the ignition key into their launch controller and started counting down, "Three, two, one . . . liftoff!"

Audrey hit the ignition button and . . . *WHOOSH!* The rocket misfired. Instead of

shooting straight up, it came barreling right over their heads. They ducked just as it shot toward Audrey's house.

As soon as the smoke cleared, Audrey glanced at the boys. They were doubled over laughing. One of them joked, "Looks like you *do* need a starter rocket!"

"You know, it's supposed to go *up*," another one said.

The tall redhead said, "Good grief. First the smashed *Saturn*, now this. You should find a new hobby!"

His friend responded, "Girls and rockets, man! They do not mix!"

Audrey looked to Gary for support, but he was staring at something on the ground. Her lip trembled. She spun on her heels and marched home. Angry tears ran down her cheeks. *Why are those boys so cruel? And why didn't Gary stand up for me?*

Her mom walked through the door behind her, holding the rocket. "Hey, kid. Does this look familiar? It almost took my head off!"

Audrey snatched it. "It doesn't work. The launch was terrible. A bunch of eighth grade boys saw it, and now I feel like a dope."

Audrey's mom put a hand on her shoulder. "You're not a dope. You're one of the best rocket scientists I know, and that's saying something." She gestured toward a photo hanging on the wall. It showed Audrey's dad standing with a group of NASA engineers. "Now fix that thing. You've still got plenty of time before the Moon landing."

Audrey stared at the rocket. She examined its pointy nose and straight fins. Everything looked fine. Then she tipped it upside down to peer at the engine cavity, the little tube that held the rocket engine.

"There it is!" She gasped.

She'd found the problem. The engine cavity was just slightly crooked. That meant that when the engine started firing, it propelled the rocket at an angle. *That* was why it had gone so haywire!

Audrey grabbed a pen and used the pointy end to reposition the engine cavity inside the rocket. She added some quick-drying glue to hold it in place. She knew she'd solved the problem, but she had to test it to be sure.

"You-were-right-Mom-bye!" she shouted as she ran outside to try another launch. This time, the rocket performed flawlessly. It soared high into the clouds.

"You fixed it!" Gary's voice rang out behind Audrey.

She turned and glared at him. "Oh, *now* you have something to say?"

"Hey, I'm sorry I got so quiet earlier. I should have stood up for you," he said.

Audrey crossed her arms over her chest.

"I think, maybe, I was just trying to act cool or something," he muttered. "They're older and . . . I don't know . . ."

"Well, don't do that again, Gary. Okay?" Audrey said.

"I promise," Gary said with a relieved smile. He looked at his watch, "Jeepers! T minus five minutes until the Moon landing! What are we still doing out here?"

They made it to Gary's house just in time. Alan and Audrey's mom were already sitting on the couch.

The TV screen showed an illustrated lunar lander wobbling through a starry sky. Then it flashed to a countdown to the landing. Twenty seconds left. Buzz Aldrin's and Neil Armstrong's voices rattled off numbers in the background. Audrey wondered what was happening in Mission Control. Her dad must be so nervous!

They all stared at the television screen. Armstrong and Aldrin gave more clipped reports. A voice from Mission Control warned them that they were nearly out of fuel. Then, finally, Armstrong said, "Houston, Tranquility base here. The *Eagle* has landed."

"THEY DID IT!" Gary howled. His mom reacted instantly. She yanked a snack tray to safety just before Gary could send it flying. Audrey jumped to her feet and whooped. Men were on the Moon!

The rest of the day passed in a blur of model rocket catalogs, snacks, and excited laughter. The astronauts had planned to do their moon walk early the following morning. But plans had changed. They were doing it that night!

Neighbors started to gather in Gary's living room around eight p.m. An hour later, it seemed like the whole community had crammed into the room. Audrey's mom took

her usual spot on the couch. Gary, Alan, and Audrey wedged themselves right in front of the TV. Gary's mom handed out coffee. At 9:56 p.m., they all watched as Neil Armstrong slowly made his way out of the lunar lander. When he stepped onto the Moon's powdery surface, he said, "That's one small step for man, one giant leap for mankind."

The crowded room was silent. For once, Gary was still. Aldrin soon joined Armstrong. He hopped down onto the Moon and exclaimed, "Beautiful! Beautiful!"

Armstrong agreed. "Isn't that something?"

The astronauts collected rocks and took photos. President Richard Nixon called them from the White House. It was the most magical thing Audrey had ever witnessed. The astronauts climbed back inside the lunar lander just after midnight. Audrey and her mom collected a sleeping Alan and headed home. But Audrey felt too excited to sleep.

When she heard her dad's car pull into the garage a bit later, she knew she had to read his notes from the day.

She waited until the house grew quiet and then snuck out to grab the flight plan. She climbed into bed with the hefty booklet and a flashlight and settled in for a night of fantastic reading.

The next thing Audrey knew, sunlight was streaming into her bedroom. She sat up groggily and heard something fall to the floor with a thump. She peered over the edge of the bed and saw it: the flight plan. She'd forgotten to put it back in her dad's briefcase! She looked at the clock. It was nearly nine a.m. Her dad was already at work!

Oh no!

Chapter 4

Audrey, We've Had a Problem

Audrey scrambled into her clothes and then ran out the door. She jammed the flight plan into her bike basket and took off, pedaling as fast as she could. Her mind raced. The astronauts were still on the Moon. They were planning to lift off in a couple of hours and would then rejoin the command module before heading back toward Earth. Her dad probably needed his flight plan to help them through all of those maneuvers. She just hoped the missing flight plan hadn't caused any problems in Mission Control.

Audrey pedaled faster. When she pulled up to the giant building, she was drenched in sweat.

"Can I help you?" an ancient-looking secretary croaked as Audrey burst into the lobby.

"My dad works here!" Audrey shouted, sprinting past. She found a door marked MOCR2 and skidded to a stop. Mission Operations Control Room 2. This was it.

She pushed the door open and slipped inside. The room was crowded with men and blinking electronics. She stared around her, wide-eyed, hardly believing what she was seeing. For a minute, Audrey nearly forgot why she was there.

The flight director stood behind a console. His arms were crossed over his chest as he quietly talked with a group of engineers. Giant displays at the front of the room showed maps

of the Moon's surface. Four rows of consoles buzzed with activity.

Right! Audrey clutched the flight plan against her chest and crept toward her dad's console.

"Hey! There's uh . . . a little girl here," a man said. He turned as if to stop her.

Audrey ignored him. Her mind flashed to the Rocketeering meeting, where she'd felt so invisible. She sure wished she was invisible now. She hurried to her dad's console and tapped him on the shoulder.

"Audrey, is everything all right? What are you doing here?" He looked pale and tired. She handed him the flight plan. He shook his head, confused.

"I fell asleep with it in my bed," she admitted. "I've . . . well, I've been reading your flight plan every night after you fall asleep."

"What were you thinking?" her dad asked

angrily. "This document is important. And it's not for kids." He sighed and rubbed his forehead. He glanced at a pair of men sitting nearby. They looked worried.

Her dad's face softened. "I'm sorry for snapping at you. It's just. . . . Audrey, we've had a problem."

She clasped a hand over her mouth. "Because I had your flight plan? I'm so sorry!"

"No, that's not it," he said. "Buzz accidentally snapped a switch off of a circuit breaker inside *Eagle* that supplies power to its engine. Without the switch, Buzz can't tell if the circuit is in the correct position. If it's not, he and Neil might not be able to lift off the Moon's surface."

Audrey gasped. "What?"

Her dad continued, "Buzz can't reach inside the breaker to check. His finger is too big for that little hole. Plus, it's an electrical surface.

He could get electrocuted." He sighed. "This is going to be tough to fix. Buzz doesn't exactly have a complete toolbox with him up there."

Audrey remembered her crooked rocket engine. "He might not have tools, but what about something he could use like a tool? Does he have a pen? He could use it to push the circuit into the right position."

A man sitting nearby leaned back in his chair and joined the conversation. "Nah, he can't do that. If he sticks a metal pen inside there and hits something live, he'll get zapped. We can't have an astronaut electrocuting himself on the Moon."

Just then, the secretary burst in. "Young lady, you cannot be in this room!" Her horn-rimmed glasses were crooked and she was out of breath. She must have hustled after Audrey. "Come with me this instant."

"Wait," Audrey said. "Just give me a second." But the secretary grabbed her arm and started tugging her toward the door. Her grip was surprisingly strong for someone so old. "What about a felt-tipped pen?" Audrey said, turning to her dad. "The felt tip isn't metal, and it won't conduct electricity. He won't get shocked!"

Her dad opened his mouth to speak, but just as he did, the secretary yanked Audrey out the door. The old woman marched Audrey all the way out to the parking lot.

Huffily, she said, "I hope you didn't touch anything in that room. Half the world is watching what happens to that crew right now. If anything goes wrong up there . . ." She shook her head. "Just go home and play. And stay out of Mission Control."

Audrey biked home slowly. She felt sick. Her dad was probably furious with her. She'd stolen his flight plan and gotten kicked out of Mission Control. And now the worst thing she could imagine was happening: Aldrin and Armstrong were in trouble.

As she pulled up to her house, an awful thought hit her: *What if the astronauts don't make it home alive?*

Chapter 5

Splashdown and Surprises

Audrey stared anxiously at the TV. It was almost one p.m. on July 21, time for Aldrin and Armstrong to leave the Moon. This, she knew, might not happen. If anything went wrong inside the *Eagle*, they'd be stuck on the surface. And there was nothing anyone would be able to do about it. If everything didn't go perfectly, they were doomed.

Alan sat nearby, playing with a model airplane and making little engine noises. "Vroom!"

Audrey shushed him. "Quiet, Alan! I need to pay attention to this."

Buzz Aldrin counted down. "Ten, nine, eight, seven, six, five . . ."

Audrey thought about the broken circuit breaker. *Had anyone in Mission Control fixed the issue?* She gulped. Her mom sat next to her on the couch.

Buzz continued, "Abort stage, engine arm, proceed."

This was it. Audrey's heart pounded wildly.

And then, the *Eagle* lifted away from the Moon. "Beautiful," Buzz said.

They'd done it! Audrey's mom squeezed her shoulder. Audrey flopped back onto the couch in relief. "Thank goodness!" she said.

Her mom laughed. "If we're this stressed out here on Earth, imagine how the astronauts must feel!"

Audrey pictured Buzz and Neil in the cramped *Eagle*. They would orbit the Moon and then meet up with the *Columbia* while looping around it. That would be incredibly difficult. The two spacecraft would have to line themselves up perfectly to dock. Then, Aldrin and Armstrong would climb into the *Columbia*, seal the space between the two vehicles, and release the *Eagle* into space. Only then could they return home to Earth.

It was a complicated, risky series of events. But for the first time that day, Audrey wasn't worried.

"They've got this," she told her mom. "It's smooth sailing from here on out."

"I hope you're right, kid," her mom said with a smile.

Audrey and her mom spent the rest of the afternoon playing board games and watching updates on the mission. Alan joined them for two rounds of Candyland, but he wandered off to his room to read comic books when Audrey suggested Scrabble.

Audrey had just scored forty-six points with the word *rendezvous* when *Eagle* docked with the *Columbia* at around four-thirty p.m. She and her mom were putting the pieces away when her dad came home.

"Dad," Audrey started. "I'm sorry about this morning."

He walked straight to the couch and collapsed into its deep cushions. Audrey bit her fingernails. She wondered if he was getting ready to lecture her.

"Audrey," he said. "I need to thank you."

Huh? she thought.

"Your idea about the pen was brilliant. We told Buzz to try it and it worked. It's very likely that you saved the mission." He cleared his throat. "You saved the crew."

Audrey's jaw dropped.

Her dad opened his briefcase and took out his flight plan. He stared at it as he spoke to her. "I know you love learning about spaceflight. I love it too. But Audrey, getting a job at NASA isn't going to be easy for you."

"You don't think I'm smart enough?" she asked.

"That's not it, kiddo." He looked at her. "Most of the people working in Mission Control are men. You'll have to fight for your seat in that room. You'll have to study hard. The topics are tricky: engineering, physics, mathematics, aviation. There will be lots of times when you'll be the only girl in your classes. You'll have to get used to speaking up when nobody wants to listen to what you have to say."

Audrey sat down next to her dad.

"I just . . ." he continued. "I suppose I tried

to steer you away from all this space stuff so you would choose an easier path. But I can see that you love this, and you're good at it. So I'm going to help you out as much as I can. Sound okay?"

Audrey grinned. "Roger."

Just then, her mom walked into the living room holding a thick book with a rocket on the cover. "What are you two talking about?" she asked.

Audrey's dad ruffled her hair. "I was just welcoming the next space scientist into the family."

"Now that's something to celebrate," her mom said with a smile.

Audrey wondered what Gary would say about all of this. She made a mental note to wait until he wasn't near anything breakable to tell him. A happy giggle escaped her lips.

After that evening, things were different between Audrey and her dad. They stayed up late every night to talk about what had happened in Mission Control, how the astronauts were doing, and what work needed to be done the following day.

When the astronauts finally splashed down in the Pacific Ocean on July 24, 1969, Audrey watched it happen in Gary's living room. But for once, she didn't feel like a little kid. She felt like an engineer in training, studying each moment.

When the next Rocketeering Club meeting rolled around, Audrey thought about what her dad had said. If she wanted to work at NASA, she'd have to fight for the chance. "Let's go again," she said.

"You sure?" Gary asked, uncertain.

"I'm sure," Audrey said.

She grabbed her repaired *Streak*, and she and Gary set off for the library. This time when they walked in, Audrey felt like she was ready for anything. But she soon realized she was wrong about that. Standing there, surrounded by admiring Boy Scouts, was Buzz Aldrin.

Audrey stopped short. Buzz looked up and smiled. "Audrey?" he said. "I've been waiting for you."

Audrey couldn't believe what she was seeing. Neither could the Boy Scouts. They looked confused.

Audrey could guess what they were thinking: *Why would the second man on the Moon want to see a little girl?*

Buzz shook Audrey's hand. "Your creative fix with that pen saved our lives. Neil and I can't thank you enough."

Gary let out a squeak and plopped into a nearby chair. Audrey wondered if he'd fainted.

"You're welcome," Audrey replied, trying to sound as professional as possible. "My pleasure."

"Now, what do you have there?" Buzz asked, pointing at Audrey's rocket.

"It's a rocket I fixed," she answered. "It wasn't launching straight, so I had to do a little problem-solving with the engine cavity." Then she smiled. "You'll never guess what tool I used."

Buzz winked and patted the felt-tipped pen sticking out of his shirt pocket. "I might have an idea."

GLOSSARY

command module (kuh-MAHND-MAHJ-OOL)—one of two vehicles made to take people to the Moon and back

console (KAHN-sole)—a desk with built-in electronic or mechanical components

flight director (FLYT dih-REKHT-tur)—the person inside Mission Control with the most authority over a space mission (Apollo 11 had four flight directors who rotated into Mission Control on shifts: Gene Kranz, Glynn Lunney, Clifford E. Charlesworth, and Gerald D. Griffin)

flight dynamics officer (FLYT dye-NAHM-iks OFF-ih-sur)—the person who monitors a spacecraft's flight path

flight path (FLYT PAHTH)—the route taken by an aircraft or spacecraft

ignition (ihg-NIH-suhn)—the device that starts something, such as an engine

lunar module (LOO-nur MAHJ-ool)—a vehicle used to travel from the Moon's orbit to the Moon's surface and back (Apollo 11's lunar module was called *Eagle*.)

orbit (OR-biht)—the curved path of an object around a planet, moon, or other celestial body

THE HISTORY BEHIND THE SPACE RACE

On May 25, 1961, President John F. Kennedy stood before a joint session of Congress and said, "I believe that this nation should commit itself to achieving the goal, before this decade is out, of landing a man on the Moon and returning him safely to Earth." It was a bold statement. NASA had only just launched its first crewed spaceflight earlier that month, when Alan Shepard flew on a fifteen-minute mission. Sending astronauts to the Moon seemed like a nearly impossible task. But the dedicated engineers, scientists, and pilots at NASA worked hard to accomplish the president's goal.

NASA's first piloted spaceflights were part of Project Mercury (1958–1963). These were a series of one-person flights. They tested a human being's ability to survive spaceflight and steer a spacecraft. Next came Project Gemini (1962–1966). These two-person missions allowed astronauts to practice longer spaceflights, do spacewalks, and learn how to dock with other spacecraft while in space.

Finally, NASA rolled out Project Apollo (1963–1972), a series of three-person flights that NASA hoped would fulfill Kennedy's dream.

The United States was not the only nation trying to land humans on the Moon. The Soviet Union (now the Russian Federation) also had a space program with the same goal. The two nations fought to achieve various space firsts before each other in a decades-long contest known as the Space Race.

The United States' Mercury and Gemini were successful projects. Unfortunately, Apollo had a rocky start. In January 1967, a fire erupted during a preflight test of Apollo 1. The three-person crew, Gus Grissom, Roger Chaffee, and Ed White, were killed. Following this tragedy, NASA put Apollo on hold while the agency investigated the fire and tried to improve its spacecraft safety.

NASA did not resume crewed flights until October 1968 with the launch of Apollo 7. This mission tested the safety of the Apollo command module in Earth's orbit. Apollo 8, 9, and 10 soon followed. These missions tested the safety of the lunar module, orbited the Moon, and allowed astronauts to further practice exiting their spacecraft in their spacesuits. These missions showed that NASA was ready for a moon landing.

Apollo 11 launched on July 16, 1969, from Cape Kennedy, Florida. It was crewed by Neil Armstrong, Edwin "Buzz" Aldrin, and Michael Collins. Its lunar module was called *Eagle*. Its command module was called *Columbia*. On July 20, about 600 million people around the world watched live on TV as Armstrong and Aldrin made the first-ever crewed Moon landing. They spent twenty-one hours on the surface of the Moon. Then, they rejoined Collins in the *Columbia*. The crew splashed down in the Pacific Ocean on July 24, 1969.

Over the following three years, five additional Apollo missions achieved Moon landings. One mission, Apollo 13, was forced to abandon a planned Moon landing after a near-catastrophic accident occurred in space. Apollo 17, in December 1972, was NASA's last lunar landing mission. As astronaut Gene Cernan prepared to leave the Moon, he said, "We leave as we came and, God willing, as we shall return: with peace and hope for all mankind."

NASA has a new Moon-landing program planned. It is named Artemis, after the Greek god Apollo's twin sister. It plans to land women and men on the Moon beginning in 2024.

ACTIVITY

Make a scale model of Earth and the Moon, and then walk the Apollo 11 flight path.

Experiment Setup

To understand the size of the Moon and its distance from Earth, try this simple activity. Make sure to set up in a wide area. Your basketball will represent Earth. The Moon, which is about ¼ the size of Earth, will be represented by the tennis ball.

Materials Needed

- regulation-sized basketball
- tennis ball
- measuring tape
- masking tape

Step 1. Make an X on the ground with your masking tape. This will represent the location of the center of Earth.

Step 2. Place the end of your measuring tape at the center of the X, and then extend it until you've reached 23 feet (7 meters).

Step 3. Use your masking tape to mark this place with an X. This will represent the location of the center of the Moon.

Step 4. Place your basketball on the first X and your tennis ball on the second X. You have now created a scale model of Earth and the Moon.

Step 5: Now, imagine that you are an astronaut and follow Apollo 11's flight path. Stand near the basketball and walk around it one and a half times. Then walk toward the tennis ball. Loop around it two and a half times, then stop to imagine you are "landing." Say a few important words for the people back home, and then get ready to return. Orbit the Moon three times, then head toward Earth. Splashdown!

ABOUT THE AUTHOR

Rebecca Rissman is an award-winning author of more than 300 books. Her work has been praised by *School Library Journal, Booklist, Creative Child Magazine* and *Learning* magazine. Rissman especially enjoys writing about American history, aeronautics, and women. She lives in Chicago, Illinois, with her husband and two daughters.

ABOUT THE ILLUSTRATOR

Jacqui Davis was born in Johannesburg, South Africa, and moved to the United Kingdom as a child. Jacqui has been producing art for children's books and board games since 2012, after studying animation at Staffordshire University. She enjoys painting everything from adorable animals to villainous wizards. Bringing life to characters is something she's always been passionate about in her work. She currently lives and works in Lytham-St-Annes, which is great for walks through the woods or ambles along the estuary.